Countdown to Thanksgiving

ISBN 978-0-545-27948-2

12 11 10 9 8 7 6   11 12 13 14 15/0

Printed in the U.S.A.   40

First Scholastic printing, October 2010

Countdown to Thanksgiving

By Jodi Huelin
Illustrated by Keiko Motoyama

SCHOLASTIC INC.
New York Toronto London Auckland
Sydney Mexico City New Delhi Hong Kong

10 family members

It's turkey day! It's family day!
With ten of us in all.
We'll celebrate Thanksgiving Day,
Give thanks, and have a ball.

9 autumn flowers

I've made a special centerpiece—
Nine flowers, bright and bold.
They've been arranged with thought and care,
The colors orange and gold.

8 steps

While the grown-ups are all cooking,
Eight steps will take us down
To the playroom in the basement—
Our place to clown around.

7 pots and pans

To prepare a feast of this size,
They'll need seven pots and pans.
But that's not all—they'll also need
A lot of helping hands!

6 holiday games

Back downstairs we play some games,
In all they number six—
Go Fish and checkers, jacks, charades,
Jump rope, and pick up sticks.

5-minute snooze

My grandma likes to rest her eyes,
"Five minutes is ideal."
At dinnertime we wake her up,
Or else she'd miss the meal!

4 cooks

Some special cooks prepare our feast;
There's four who do the job:
Cousin Meg and Auntie Marge,
My dad and Grandpa Bob.

3 yummy pies

For dessert we will have some pie—
Three tasty homemade treats!
Apple, cherry, and pumpkin too,
All baked by Uncle Pete!

2 dueling televisions

In my house it's a tradition,
To turn on two TVs.
There's football for the sports fans,
And parades for kids like me!

1 golden turkey

And best of all, we save for last,
One very special treat
A golden turkey carved with care,
Hooray—it's time to eat!

I'm glad you came along to share
The fun along the way.
Celebrating with my family
Happy Thanksgiving Day!

Thanksgiving

Count down to a special day with family, friends, and fun!

Share in one family's celebration while counting down from ten family members to one big Thanksgiving feast! Little gobblers will come back for seconds (and thirds) to read about the sights and smells of Turkey Day!

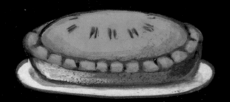

www.scholastic.com

This edition is available for distribution only through the school market.

ISBN 978-0-545-27948-2

EAN

9 780545 279482